MW01097771

Praise for THE LITTLE CAT THAT ZOOMED

"The best book I've ever read!"
-Mom

"Destined to be a classic."
-Neighbor dog, Flo

"Must read book of the year!"
-@sugarpodell
#shamelessplug

"Every library should have this book."
-My school's librarian

The Little Cat that Zoomed
Copyright © 2021 by Ashley Podell and Eyal Podell

All rights reserved. No part of this publication may be reproduced, distributed, or transmitted in any form or by any means, including photocopying, recording, or other electronic or mechanical methods, without the prior written permission of the author and publisher, except in the case of brief quotations embodied in critical reviews and certain other noncommercial uses permitted by copyright law. For permissions requests, contact the publisher at www.east26thpublishing.com

Library of Congress Cataloging-in-Publication data is available
ISBN: (Hardback) 978-1-955077-29-3 | (Paperback) 978-1-955077-30-9 | (eBook) 978-1-955077-31-6

10 9 8 7 6 5 4 3 2 1
First printing edition 2021

East 26th Publishing
Houston, TX

www.east26thpublishing.com

THE LITTLE CAT THAT ZOOMED

Written by Ashley & Eyal Podell
Illustrated by Rebecca Montoya Dieppa

EAST 26TH
PUBLISHING

FROM THE AUTHORS

For Oren and Guy — our favorite muses — for showing us that we can find opportunities for growth in our greatest challenges.

For my Mom, Jan, for telling me that I really should write this book and for the endless love and support.

FROM THE ILLUSTRATOR

For my incredible son, Noah, for cracking open my heart.

Sugar the cat had a very nice life.

She lived in a nice house...

with a nice family...

Everything was nice.

Sugar had fun when the family was home.

They had so much love to give her.

When the family was away, Sugar kept herself busy.

Eating...

Playing...

Bathing...

Making friends...

When the family came home,
Sugar was happy to be with them.

Until the day they came home...

and stayed.

The family was everywhere!

She had no privacy!

She couldn't see her friend as well.

There were things all over her bathing area.

It was impossible to keep things normal.

She couldn't do anything the way she wanted to.

All the changes made Sugar angry.

Then something unexpected happened. The boy brought Sugar to his class for show and tell.

Sugar loved
hearing all the kids
say hi to her from the
magic rectangle.

Sugar enjoyed going to school with the boy.

Each day she learned
something new.

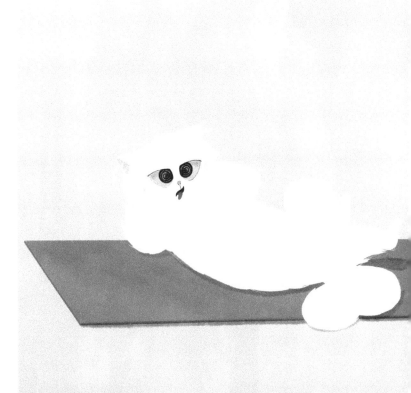

There was so much to see in the magic rectangle that Sugar's imagination

RAN WILD!

HOLLYWOOD

NORTH AMERICA

SOUTH AMERICA

Sugar saw
the whole world in the
magic rectangle.

EUROPE

ASIA

AFRICA

ANTARCTICA

AUSTRALIA

And at night, when everyone was asleep...

Sugar learned even more!

But the best lesson Sugar learned is that sometimes our biggest challenges...

give us opportunities to grow.

Eventually, the family went back to school and work.
But this time, Sugar had new things to fill her day.

AUTHORS

Ashley and Eyal Podell live in southern California with their two children and pet cat (third child), Sugar. Like many parents, 2020's extended quarantine forced them to get creative. After dabbling in sourdough, they decided to channel their energy into children's books. This one is based on Sugar's true story.

ILLUSTRATOR

Rebecca Montoya Dieppa is a new mom and artist living in Los Angeles. Having worked many jobs in the creative arts, she is thankful to have had the opportunity to live a fully artistic life — one which is ever-expanding. Currently she's been very busy looking at the world through the eyes of her son, whom she lovingly refers to as "her best creation yet."

CPSIA information can be obtained
at www.ICGtesting.com
Printed in the USA
LVHW070947230921
698555LV00003B/4